GRANDPA

AND

THE

COMPUTER

By James W. Hart
A Descendant of William Shakespeare

Grandpa and the Computer

ISBN: 1-893798-18-6

Library of Congress Cataloging-in-Publication Data

Hart, James W., 1918-
  Grandpa and the computer / written by James W. Hart.
      p. cm. -- (Grandpa and the computer ; 1)
Includes index.
  ISBN 1-893798-17-8 (alk. paper)
 1. Computer literacy. 2. Internet and the aged. 3. Computers and the
aged. I. Title. II. Grandpa and the computer (Series) ; 1.
  QA76.9.C64 H37 2001

                                       2001005026

Series title: Grandpa and the Computer
Series number: 1

NewMedia Publishing
31 Franklin Turnpike
Waldwick, NJ 07463, USA
www.newmediapublishing.com
SAN: 253-293X

DEDICATION

This book is dedicated to my family,
and to all the good people of this world.

"I don't understand #11...
Thou shalt not be obscene
on the Internet."

TABLE OF CONTENTS

FOREWORD

The author was 82 years old when he learned to use a computer. It took him eight months of trial and error to do so. He did it on his own. So can other grandmas, grandpas, and folks who grew up without one. What's more - they can now become instant experts, following in his footsteps.

This book makes it really easy for them to communicate with their family, as well as their extended family - the world at large. They can roam all over the Internet; get answers quickly; find new pen pals; even play with others, thousands of miles away.

There are many other things they can do with a computer. There are also many kinds of computers, other than what is described in this book, which is a PC with Windows® from Microsoft. Apple Macintosh and iMac® are also very popular and easy to use. Linux® is another one, moving up rapidly. Fortunately, it doesn't really matter which one you get. They work the same way, even if they look somewhat different. You may have the Netscape browser to surf the Internet and for email. Or AOL, that is America OnLine. Again, they do the same thing, basically the same way as what is written about here. So what you learn will be useful, regardless of the computer you have.

You can find the author's web page link on the last page, in case you want to check in with him for an email chat. We'll be glad to respond, as it will mean you've mastered this "monster," called a computer - which is what this book is all about.

Steven Kingsley
Publisher

7

INTRODUCTION

This book about computers can be easily understood by just about anyone. It conveys the style of how the author speaks and thinks, translating his views from the heart.

As such, it most certainly is a one of a kind book. After you've read it, you should come to the same conclusion.

Finally, this book was written for your enjoyment and to help you see, through the eyes of the eighty-two years old author, what he means for you to learn in a simple way.

Terry Barnhart
A neighbor of the author

"To upgrade or not to upgrade, that is the question!"

CHAPTER 1

THE LIFE OF THE AUTHOR

This is a true story about James W. Hart and the computer, or as some Grandpas might call it "the monster." But, before I get started on how simple it is to learn about this thing called the computer, I want to tell you a little about myself and a little bit about my life.

I was born in a little town in West Virginia on the first day of March 1918 to very humble parents. This was toward the end of World War I, so I guess you could call me a WW I baby. As I started to grow up and got into my teenage years I finally finished the eighth grade and I was very smart, or at least I thought I was. So I went to work for fifty cents a day but I thought I was worth more than that and kind of smarted off to my parents. Dad said to me, "James, you won't mount to a hill of beans." That was the first setback of my young life. I said to myself (because I couldn't say it to my Dad), "Well James, you've got a head on your shoulders and a little gray matter inside it, so use it." That's the first time I had thought that if I was going to prove anything to myself, not to my parents, I'd have to take the "common sense approach." For the rest of my life that's what I did. Never forgetting my background, but always looking ahead at the ground in front of me. I finished school knowing the teachers were not any smarter than me on account of their education; hence I was able to use my common sense approach there too.

As the years passed I was like every other red-blooded American. I got married to a beautiful red headed girl and, as we loved each other, it became apparent that we would have a family and you know something, we did. We had six wonderful children, eighteen grandchildren, and twenty great grand children. At this point in our life, after sixty years of marriage, my wife passed away and left me very lonely. By this time we also had arrived at the computer age. Why I mention all this is because my oldest son had four children. The second child's name is Tam. So, that is the start of Grandpa and the computer.

Tam called me one day and said, "Grandpa, I'm going to get you a computer." I asked her, "What is a computer?" She replied, "Grandpa you surely know what a computer is." I said to her, "I've heard of some kind of a contraption, so if you want to get me one, I won't turn it down, but who's going to run it?" She said, "Grandpa, you are." I thought, "My God, what am I going to do now?" But I was never one to back down on something that was going to be given to me.

The younger generation today is very highly educated, where-as we Grandpas didn't have a chance to really get an education. We learned the hard way on how to do anything. So, we had to use common sense for everything we did. In the computer age, I'll show all that will listen, that even us old timers can learn to use the computer without any lessons. To all you Grandpas out there, you take up a big part of the population of this great country called the United States of America. Why should we let all the young people take all this fun away from us? We can do anything they can. All we have to do is do it, or one day we will be put out to pasture. My simple way will surely give you encouragement. You might not know now what a computer is, but after you read my book you'll have nothing to worry about, and have fun using it.

In the third chapter I'll tell you how I got started on this monster called the computer. The word for computer means: Come put her to work. You will see, my step-by-step plan shows that we are not an old, outdated bunch of Grandpas. Just because technology moved in does not mean that we Grandpas are moved out. It does mean though, that we go with the flow. So this thing moved in, it doesn't mean we move out. What it does mean is that we can handle anything that technology brings our way. That includes this monster called the computer. Grandpas, and grandmas don't need to be afraid of this monster. We just need to get one, conquer it and have a barrel of fun. It thinks it is smarter than we are, but to tell you the truth it is dumb. It has no brain; no sense of direction, and it only puts out what we put in. I'm going to show you how I outsmarted this thing, and had fun doing so.

Get ready for the true story of how I went all over the world and never left my home. I saw things with my eyes that even I, James W. Hart, would never have believed, until I conquered this thing called the computer. You will have to get a computer and try it for yourself. I can give you my step-by-step plan on how to do it the simple way. So hang on, and let's try this the James W. Hart way - THE SIMPLE WAY.

"I taught him how to type W-O-O-F.
Now he can bark at strangers all over the Internet!"

CHAPTER 2

MY NOSY NEIGHBOR

My nosy neighbor saw my granddaughter Tammy, and my son-in-law Bill drive up with this computer, and take it into my house. So, over he comes and asks me a question, "James, (of course we were friends) what in the hell (his words not mine) are you up to?" I looked at him kind of puzzled, as if he thought I was from outer space or just went kind of crazy. I said, "Joe, what does it really matter to you what I'm up to?"

"Well James, why are you always trying to think of ways to keep from working?" I replied to my neighbor, "You know Joe, every Grandpa has a head on his shoulder and we are going to use it for something besides a hat rack. Do you, Joe, think that no one has a brain but you? God gave every Grandpa in this country a chance to do something when we become senior citizens." Of course he had seen them bring the computer into my home that's why he was questioning me about this whole thing. Talk about being nosy! But I wasn't going to let a nosy, troublesome guy ruin my day with these dumb questions, or even discourage me in any way from what I was getting ready to learn, and do without any help from anyone. I had made up my mind, and I knew it would be hard, but I figured the harder the better. Then, when I learned this thing I would never forget how much of a challenge it was.

I also knew my neighbor didn't know anything about the computer, or he would not have come over in the first place. Not only that, I also knew he didn't have any common sense. By this time Tammy, and Bill had this thing set up and ready to go. They came outside and said to me, "Grandpa it's all set up now, it's your baby and we don't mean maybe. It's yours to conquer."

They said, "Have fun," and left.

So I asked my nosy neighbor, "Do you want to go in and see what they set up for me?" You know something - this guy never hesitated to go in to look at this thing. We went into the room together to look at the computer. I'll admit I was a nervous wreck by this time. I didn't know a thing about it, and I was sure this guy was going to ask me a bunch more questions that I probably couldn't answer. To my surprise he didn't ask me anything. He looked like he was in a daze. He glanced at the computer then he looked at me.

He walked to the door, and then he walked back looking puzzled. He said, "James, I've lived by you for thirty years, and I never thought in my wildest dreams you had the nerve to try something like this." I said, "Joe, just because I'm eighty-two years old doesn't mean I'm for the rocking chair yet. I'm going to prove to the world and also to you, neighbor, that you don't have to be smart, and that all my life I never was afraid to try anything. After all, my granddaughter gave this to me, and if she wanted me to keep happy, and cheerful I wasn't about to let her down. So you see Joe, all my life I've used common sense, so that's what I'll stand on now." He turned and said, "James, good luck because you'll need it." After showing him out I walked back into my house. By this time I was exhausted from letting my neighbor get under my skin. So, I sat down in my easy chair to relax from all the excitement this guy had caused me, and before I started my journey through this thing and all the technology that goes with it. So I decided to rest my nerves for a while.

You might think I'm going the long way here, to get to the stage of learning. What I really wanted you to see from this experience was how easy it is to give up on anything we Grandpas, - and Grandmas too - want to do.

16

In the next chapter we are going all the way with my experiences from turning my computer on, up until I learned all that I know now. I will tell you how I got started on it, and how scared I was at first to even turn it on. Not knowing if I would ruin it, get lost in all the roadways and byways that were inside of it, or completely get disgusted and kick it out of my house.

It will be a true story mixed with humor of how I made plenty of mistakes. On the other hand (did you know we had two hands?), I had lots of fun doing it all by myself. So the next chapter will definitely be Grandpa and the computer. Hang on to your seat, and let's travel every road in this thing.

"NEVER HIT THE SAME KEY OVER AND OVER...THEY HATE THAT!"

CHAPTER 3

GRANDPA AND THE COMPUTER, HILLBILLY STYLE

I'm going to tell you my true story about learning the computer, as I myself started out completely ignorant of anything like this since I was born. I spent countless hours pulling my hair out and learning this thing, by not being afraid to mess up.

First, I sat down in my chair, in front of the computer and looked at the black screen for a few minutes. Then I fumbled around all over the computer looking for the switch. I finally found it, so I turned it on. I never heard such a commotion, inside that thing, as it was coming on. I saw all kinds of things flashing on the screen. When it finally stopped there was a screen full of what they call icons. One icon said *My Computer,* well I already knew that, it certainly was mine. I looked at the rest of them; *My Documents, Network Neighborhood, Real Player, Net Zero, Windows Explorer, Acrobat Reader, Family Tree, Internet Explorer, Outlook Express, Games, Downloads,* and *Online Services.*

Down in the left-hand corner, there was a word in bold letters that said *Start.* I won't go into the rest of the words on the two bars on the bottom but I will tell you that the right side of the bar had the time. I guess they wanted you to know how long you've been working. I looked the screen over and figured I better start where it says *Start.* Oh yes, I had better mention the mouse. It is connected to the keyboard. Thank God for that little mouse. It could get you out of more trouble than any other rodent. I believe they called it a mouse because nothing else could go through this maze but a mouse.

19

So I clicked on *Start* and up popped this line of words; *Programs, Find, Run, Help, Log Off lefty* and *Shut Down.* I didn't want to shut down, I wanted to go through this thing but I didn't know how to get back to the first screen. But I accidentally clicked on *Start* again and was back where I had started. I saw one icon that kind of caught my eyes. It said *Internet Explorer.*

Well I thought, I'm on the Internet so why not explore. I clicked on it and nothing happened, so I clicked two times and it worked. It went to the next screen where it looked like every word in the English language was on it. But what caught my eye this time was *Mail*. I clicked on it and that brought up other words; *Read Mail, New Message, Send Page, and Read News* (see how confusing it is). I clicked *Read Mail.* Well there was no mail but how could there be, I hadn't written anything yet. Now I did know I had an email address because my daughter had taped it on a little piece of paper to my computer. So I called my son and asked him to email me to see if I could answer. I gave him my email address and he said he would. I waited a few minutes and sure enough my computer told me that I had mail. I looked over the screen and clicked on the button that said *Answer.* Sure enough I had received his message with his address on it. Under his address, where it said *Subject,* I wrote "testing". After I wrote my letter I saw where it said *Send.* So I clicked on *Send* and the email was on its way. Since I was becoming fairly comfortable with the mail part of this technological world, I figured I would play with the email stuff for a while.

I thought to myself, "This isn't so bad learning this stuff." Pretty soon I started receiving email from all over the world and after eight months I became an email wizard. How all these people got my address is kind of a mystery to me but what the heck, life is a mystery. But you know something, every email I received was from a woman, not a single email was from a man (see, life is a bowl of jelly).

20

So let's go on with my learning experience. I realized that this computer must have a brain because time and time again it tried, and usually succeeded in leading me down roads that I couldn't get back from. It forced me to shut down and start up countless times. It seemed that this thing was just like a woman trying to mess up my mind. I spent hundreds of hours messing up, but in the end you'll see how I conquered this thing. I was determined to whip this thing all by myself; consequently I went back to the second screen where I saw *Search*. Well, I thought I'd try *Search* out with my little mouse. I clicked it and got a screen with a blank line having no clue as to what it meant. I had never even heard of a web site, so I thought I would put something in there. And this was the start of my search.

22

Chapter 4

PEN PALS

I typed in "pen pals" and to my surprise pen pals came up on the screen with a list of web sites that had pen pals. I found out one thing, if you put the arrow (which is also called a cursor) over spots you want to go, it shows you a hand with a finger pointing at that link. So I picked one link at a time and jumped in with both feet (remember this was all free). Each site had pen pals listed from all over the world. I thought, well I'm pretty lonely so I'm going to try some of those pen pals. I found out another thing too: Anything you want to do like this, the company always wants you to register. They want you to give your name, email address, if you are a man or woman and what age you are looking for. So you see, if you use common sense, the computer will lead you pretty well where you want to go.

I picked out one site that looked pretty good to me. I entered what the computer asked for. I put in that I was a man in my early seventies, looking for women between thirty-five and seventy (see, I lied about my age to see what I could find). You also had to state what country you wanted, or if it was in the United States. They also wanted to know the state where you were to conduct your search. So I picked Ohio, anywhere in the state. Why I picked this state, is because I live in Ohio. Every woman that was listed in Ohio, in that age bracket, came up on the screen. It gave their names, height, weight and their hobbies. So I picked out three of them who looked pretty good to me. I didn't pick out any that wanted to travel. But I'll admit I picked out the youngest ones I thought would write, and be interested in me. See, deep down inside I wanted more than a pen pal. And to tell you the truth, I found out they did too.

The company told me to send the emails through them. They in turn gave the person the email but not my email address. So these women had to email me back through the company. They said there were crazies out there and this would protect me. I wasn't having any success because the company controlled us. So I got tired of that stuff and I wrote an email to all three women, giving everyone of them my email address, and of course I had to go through the company. I figured they wouldn't let it go through but they said they didn't read the email, so I took the chance. Right away I got an email from all three of them and did we have fun emailing each other. After several weeks two of them got pretty serious about me. I want to tell you that I was not a married man, I was a widower, and so I was clear of getting into serious trouble. But what I did do was, I told them the truth about my age. I told them I was eighty-two years old, not in my seventies, and I was just having fun. They said they didn't care, age was just a number. Now I knew they were lying. Well enough of my courtship - let's get back to learning. The next chapter will be mostly on *Search.*

Chapter 5

MORE ON EXPLORING *SEARCH*

I stayed on *Search* to see what else I could get into. I wrote in everything from women, religion, antiques, celebrities, ways to make money, new and used cars, buying, and selling, etc. Now I'll admit I got into all kind of messes on many of these trips in and out of these searches. Some of the time you could back out of them with no problem by pressing the *Back* button. Many times I would press the *Back* button, and for some outlandish reason it would send me to some other web site many times removed and having nothing in common with the original site I had visited. At times it seemed like every time I got out of that site another one would pop up to replace it. I would eventually get so flustered I'd just shut down the computer and start all over again. You see this computer is like a big highway, with thousands of off ramps to thousands of other roads. So if you didn't really know what ramp to turn off you would naturally get lost, and boy did I get lost, countless times.

Once I was working my head off and to my surprise, I saw a flashing light on the screen. It said: "You have committed an illegal act. Your computer will shut down in twenty seconds." My Lord, I thought I had committed a serious crime and I would go to jail, or maybe to the penitentiary for life. So, as quick as I could, I hurried and shut off the computer before it could shut itself down, and maybe the authorities wouldn't know who committed the crime. I figured that since I was on the Internet everyone would know I had committed this act. After I shut it down I stumbled out of the room as quickly as possible, took a nerve pill and decided to leave the contraption alone for a while to see if anyone was going to call or maybe come and get me.

"It's right here in your own handwriting.
You didn't ask for Linux, you asked for Linus!"

After about three or four hours I figured I was safe, no one had caught me, so I went back to the computer and started it up again. I had been keeping notes on a note pad of everything I had been doing for future reference but I had no idea what to write down about what had just happened. To this day, I'm still not sure what it was I had done.

If I had known more about web sites I might have been able to find what I was looking for much quicker. However, I was able to find things with my search method, it just took a little longer. I had heard that you could make purchases over the Internet with a credit card and there was a book a friend of mine had told me about that I thought would be interesting, so I decided to look for it. I typed in the word "books" and there were literally millions of sites pertaining to that subject, so I realized that maybe I should try to narrow my search down. I typed in the title of the book and the author's name, and found it for sale at the first site I went to. All I had to do was to type in my credit card number. I was a little worried about sending that kind of information through cyberspace but my son reassured me that this type of info would be all right to send because it would be encrypted as it was being transferred to them.

I must tell you that while you are searching for things on the Internet, it is pretty darn important to type in the correct word or words. One day I was searching for a book that had the word "best" in it. I somehow must have typed in "breast" by mistake. I clicked, then realizing the mistake I said to myself "Oh boy, what have I done!" I hadn't noticed what exactly had happened, so I clicked on one of the choices and I saw right away I was in uncharted waters. Before my eyes was something that Adam and Eve would not have seen. Pictures that I couldn't take, a disgrace even to me. Up in the left hand corner there is a X to eliminate that window, so I pressed it but the more I clicked the more pictures kept coming.

The more I clicked the worse it got. They must not want you to get out once you are in. I was so embarrassed that my face turned purple. Finally I clicked home and got out of that ungodly mess. I remembered, next time, to be more careful. I just had to tell you that whatever you put in will come out. Now we can go on.

Chapter 6

LEARNING FROM MISTAKES

In this chapter there will be many little learning experiences that I fought through and some of them may not seem like much to someone that is a professional, but as I said before you don't have to be a professional. But when you are an eighty-two year old Grandpa, sometimes your way can be the best way and I think it is. If you remember, when I started this story, I didn't even know how to turn the computer on. So this was, by far, the biggest challenge of my life but I had lived through many a challenge through all these many years (the same as all Grandpas, and Grandmas had). Making lots of mistakes, and a lot of choices along the way. The old saying is, you always learn from your mistakes. If ever there was a true saying, this was it. In learning this thing, I also had to make choices of what to do and where to go next. Needless to say, in the beginning I made more bad choices than good ones. In the next few chapters you will see how this will pay off for every Grandpa or anyone that wants a computer.

I remember I was about a month into learning and somehow I dragged the arrow across, then up and down the screen. I'm talking about the screen with all the icons and the bars on it, which is the first screen you see when you turn the computer on. I must have also messed up the second screen, which is my *Home Base*. It is Hometown Ohio on my computer. Your *Home Base* could be different from mine. What I didn't realize was that there were two Hometown Ohio browsers open on my computer instead of one. But just one of them is mine, the one from which I navigate. The other one is different and for the life of me I don't know why it is on there.

The bottom half is completely different from the one I use. Well, let's take the first screen first and how I had it so messed up I couldn't believe what I had done.

I finally figured out how I had put myself in this mess. I was moving the arrow across and up and down the screen, while holding down the left button of the mouse without realizing what I was doing. I kept holding it down until I dragged every icon off the screen. I had dragged one of the bars on the bottom left to the top of the screen and it was upside down. The other bar I had dragged over on the right side. You talk about a mess, I had created a monster and I didn't know what to do about it. After about four hours playing around with this thing, it looked to me like I was making it worse. I got some of the icons back by dragging them back one at a time. I worked and worked and thought, "James, how could you have been so careless to do such a thing." I finally dragged the bar from the right side to the bottom of the screen but it was in the wrong place. I looked at the bar on the top of the screen, which was still upside down. Then, I just about lost my head. I started to scream, "The hell with it all!" But something clicked in my head that seemed to say, "Hey listen James, you believe in God don't you? Do not use that kind of language." So I quit for a while, to calm my nerves.

After a few hours I was back at it, having thought things out. I took my mouse and went to the upside down bar on the top and clicked on the bar and I saw that it had a little long arrow pointing whichever way I wanted to drag it. So I dragged it down around the right side of the screen and got it turned around so it was right side up. Then I dragged it to the bottom where it belonged. And you know something, when I got it in place the other bar, which I already had down there, somehow fell right in line where it was supposed to be.

Now, to finish my job, I had to drag the icons where they were in the first place. I had accomplished my work, and this screen was in order and ready to go. Once more I had used common sense and a lot of luck, but I wasn't done yet. I had one more task to do, and that was to get my *Home Page* back instead of the one that was there, because I couldn't use my computer without my *Home Base*. I clicked on the *Internet Explorer* icon and it went to Hometown Ohio - but of course the wrong one. Across the top of the screen in the web browser is this bar with all kinds of words to click on. I kept clicking on every word but none of them helped, until I had only one left to click. It didn't even look logical because the word was *History*. I clicked on it and to my amazement it brought up, on the left side of the screen, all kind of lines to click on. As I looked at all of them right before my eyes I about had a heart attack. It said - *Hometown Ohio You*. I clicked on it with my mouse and up came my *Home Page,* big as life.

I had done it. Everything was back in order. I took my right hand and shook my left hand and congratulated myself for a job well done. I was never dumb enough to ever do that again. I sure made a note of this terrible mistake, to never do that again. Another little thing I learned was two ways to get to *Search,* I've already told you the one way. On my home page there are lots of things to go out on, which I won't mention but this *Search* was on this page. So, that makes two ways to search and it expands *Search.* Just follow the little red line and it will take you to the next chapter where you will find a little more about my learning. Then the scene will change to an interlude, then into how to, and how not to, run the computer.

Chapter 7

LEARNING THE DO'S AND DON'TS

This is a chapter on a few things that you don't need to do and some things that you do need to do. Now remember, I've been through eight months of training myself and now I'm ready to tell everyone how to do it and not have to go through basic training. Keep in mind that this is my idea of teaching you from my personal experience. From an eighty-two-year old Grandpa that most people would think should be back on the shelf. The do's and don'ts will keep you all out of trouble. It really will be trouble free. So Grandpas and Grandmas, if you want something useful to do, take this advice and run with it, and enjoy yourself to the fullest.

In fact, I'm going to put a little warning here so you will not forget. Here is one thing you must do for protection if there is a storm in your area. Be sure to shut down your computer until the storm passes by. I didn't know that, so one evening lightening from a storm hit the wires, and knocked out my computer. I was also on the cable TV, and it threw me off the line so it stopped me from working. I turned my computer back on and luckily nothing was damaged in it, except it wouldn't go online. What I mean is, if it doesn't go online you can't work on the Internet. The modem wasn't working. The same thing would have happened, had I been hooked up to the phone line. So I called the cable TV company and told them what had happened. They checked and said everything was OK on their end. "It's on your end," they said. I asked them what I could do. They told me to unplug the modem for about thirty seconds then plug it back in. If that doesn't fix it, unplug the whole system from the wall receptacle and wait at least five minutes, then turn everything back on. I did that and everything worked.

"I NEED A BETTER WORD PROCESSOR FOR MY HUSBAND.
ONE THAT WILL CORRECT HIS SPELLING, GRAMMAR AND OPINIONS."

Let's talk about the icons on the first screen. First the ones you don't need, they're just there to make the screen more attractive, I believe. Let's take the icon - *Games*, this is one icon you will want on your computer. When you get tired of working just click on *Games,* and play your favorite ones. Relax and have fun.

Windows Explorer, now this icon is important if you want to find things, but to me it is worthless, just a pretty icon on the screen. Icon - *Acrobat Reader 4.0*, why would they even put this one on the screen, except for looks, I believe. Are you beginning to get the picture about icons? Icon - *On Line Services*, this is where you can find a lot of things out there on the Net, but I have other ways to do the same thing. Don't need to use it. Icon - *Network Neighbor-hood*, you can use if you are on a network in the office, or at home. Icon - *My Computer*, I don't use it at all. I store things that I want anyway.

There are icons you will use sometimes, and icons you will use all the time. Icon - *Recycle Bin* is where things that you don't want any more go, when you delete them. You can also bring them back from there, if there was one you wanted, or you can remove them permanently from the bin. This will clear files off your hard drive and give you more space so you won't have to worry about running out of room on the computer. Icon - *MSN*, you can get Internet and email access from this one but I don't use it either. Why? Because I go the easy way. Icon *Download* allows you to download anything from here. If someone sends you a greeting or anything that's important, you can download it to see or hear it. You can even download music or anything else you want to through this icon.

Icon - *Outlook Express*, is the most important icon on your computer. Now I understand that on other computers *Outlook Express* will have another name, such as *AOL Mail, Netscape Messenger* or *Eudora Mail*. But you will know and if you don't know, ask if they are the same, then you'll be OK.

This is the program that lets you send and receive email and it will enable you to get in touch with anyone in the world. More about that in Chapter 9.

We talked about *Windows Explorer* but I wanted to comment a little further. When you click on this icon you bring up, on the left side of your screen, *Windows*, *Program Files* and others, but don't worry about this window because you really can stay away from it ("Don't worry, be happy.") One more icon that I really like is *Real Player*. You can click on *Real Player* (remember all this is done with that poor little rodent, the mouse), and it will bring up the CD player, so you can listen to music all day. You can also use *QuickTime*, or *Windows Media Player*. But if you want to work on the computer while you listen to music, you don't have to go this route. On the front of your computer, toward the top, there is a button you can push in, and the holder for the CD comes out. Place your CD in there, then touch it to go back in. Your CD will start to play automatically. Listen to music while you work. Your computer may have different icon names but they do the same work. We have arrived to the Interlude chapter. Remember - nine months have gone by for me. So we will be in this chapter between my learning, and teaching my way as a Grandpa.

Chapter 8

INTERLUDE

This is the interlude chapter between my learning the computer and the mistakes I made. Reading about them here will spare you from making the same mistakes. This is also about my teaching the best way, so you can go through the running of the computer trouble free. To go from the beginning to as far as you want to go, and do the things you want to do with your computer without having the headaches that I had.

I believe, that because of all of those eight months of learning everything by myself, I can help you. Remember, as I've said before, this is through the eyes of an eighty two-year old Grandpa. It will be different from what a child or a young person would tell you to do, but their way is so complicated you could never learn the easy way. So through my experience, what I learned by myself, I can give you the best and easiest way to have fun. It will get you through the computer and learn the easy way without spending a lot of money on costly lessons that won't help you as much as taking my plan of learning. All you have to do is to take my book and start working on the computer immediately, without someone standing over you, and making a nervous wreck out of you. Those educated teachers tell you to make every move their way. Then you forget about half of what they tell you to do anyway.

I'm going to tell you what to start on first and what to continue with right on through. This way it will be easy. In the summary chapter I'm going to give you a bird's eye view, and a step by step plan to success. If you don't think this book is witty and humorous, and also the right way of learning my method, then it is probably not for you.

"My son burps into the microphone and e-mails it to his friend across town. What amazing things does *your* kid do with *his* computer?"

But before you come to any conclusions, read the rest of the book. Then if you are still not satisfied, give it to a friend. She or he might just like it. As I previously told you, we make choices of everything we do in life. As always, if we make the wrong choice we cannot go back and change it. It will affect us the rest of our lives. You have two choices in learning the computer. One way is my plan from my perspective. Or, if you want to do it the hard way, you can spend a lot of money taking costly lessons. In the end, you will be no better off. Read on and hear my teaching.

Chapter 9

MY TEACHING PLAN

This chapter is about teaching you how to run the computer the easy way, and to bypass all the things the educated ones tell you to do. My way will be easy, fruitful and fun, rather than hard and complicated. We will start from the beginning, after the computer is set up and ready to go. The truth is, you should have others, who really know how - preferably someone in your family - do the setup and connecting to the Internet. These are not easy tasks in most cases. Once connected, you can get onto the Internet in different ways. While I use the service provided by my cable TV company, you may have AOL (America OnLine), or the telephone company itself for that.

So let's start by sitting down for the first time, and learning how to run it my way. Turn on the computer with the on/off switch. The first screen that appears will be the one with all the *Program* icons on it. Don't be afraid when you see all the icons. Just double-click on the one I tell you to, and you will be on your way to success. Do you remember when you were young, and you wrote your first letter to your girl friend or your boy friend? It took two or three weeks to get an answer back. Well, the computer just took the old way, and made it very fast to communicate with friends, family - even the whole world.

Here is the first lesson. Now that you have your computer on, and the icons up, move your mouse so as to place the arrow on the icon - *Internet Explorer, Netscape, or AOL,* and double-click rather quickly. This will take you to your *Home Page*. From here you can get your web browser to go to what we will do next.

The first place to go would be to click on *Mail* - that will show you *Read Mail*. Click on *Read Mail*, which will put you into your email program. The bar on the top of the window will say; *New Mail, Reply, Reply All, Forward, Print, Delete and Address*.

Let's take *New Mail* now. Click on this one to email someone for the first time. Get a person's email address so you can email him or her, then they will answer you via email. Then, to answer them back, click on *Answer* and write your letter and click on *Send*. If you have two or more letters you would want to send to different people you could click on *Reply All.* This will send all the letters at the same time. If you get a *Forward* from someone and you like what it's about, and you would like your friends to see it, just click on *Forward*, then on *Send*. Everything so far is in order. *Print* is part of your email program, so if you have something someone has sent you, and you want to keep it to hang on the wall or put in your file, just hit *Print*, and it will print it out for you. *Delete* will remove the messages you don't need anymore, and will make room for more email. Click on the ones you want to delete; click *Delete* and they will be moved into your *Recycle Bin*. If it is something you will never want to save, after a month or so go into your *Recycle Bin*, and delete it from there. This will also give you more room on your hard drive.

Address, this is your *Address Folder* where you will want to keep all the addresses of your email friends, even companies, or government agency workers you want to be able to communicate with. The way you do this is to click on *Address*. This will bring up your *Address Book* or *Folder*. How you enter all the addresses you want? By clicking on *New*, *New Contact* will come up. Write in their name, email address and phone number if you know it, but the phone number is not necessary. Then click *OK* - now they are in your address book.

42

If you get an email from someone you don't know, or maybe a company, be careful before you open it. It could contain a virus and ruin everything on your hard drive. If it looks suspicious, delete it.

Always remember your password, email address, and computer name, unless your computer is set to give them to you automatically, in order to let you go directly in. Mine is set to do that. Remember, your email address is the most important for what you will do. If you want a short cut to your email program, just click twice on *Outlook Express* and you are there, instead of going through *Internet Explorer* or your *Home Page*, thereby saving time.

I put all this right in here, because it is important to show you how to do these things to keep you up to date with your computer. You can find out more about them in the *Useful Things to Know* section, starting on page 51.

Let's go back to email. Say if you want to send an email to CNN, or CBS, or anyone else. Get their email address, and voice your opinion, gripe, or anything else that's on your mind. Keep running this email program until you are good at it. Then you can branch out to other things. All this time you can play your *Real Player* until you are tired of music, but if you have soothing music on it will keep your nerves settled.

The next step, and really the only one you will ever need, is *Search*. You can go to *Search* from your *Home Page* or from an icon on the bottom of your browser page. If you don't know one web site, don't worry; it's just as well. It's more fun to use words, that is what I do and I'm going to tell you to do the same. This is my step-by-step plan to success. For example, if you want to visit any country in the world just type in the country you want to visit. There will be one web site after another to go to, in order to find out everything about that country, and every picture, history, city, you name it, it's all there.

If you want to find anything, *Search* is the answer. Say if you want to see Big Ben in England, type in "Big Ben." Forget all the other icons that take you to the same place and just go on *Search*. It's much easier this way, and you're not worrying about all those icons. This is the simplest way to use the Internet with fewer problems. You'll find it so easy because you can follow the choices the computer gives you, and arrive at the things you need and want. It just takes practice and common sense. The road is there - you just follow it. Use your email icon to get into your email program; then use any one of the *Searches,* and you can scan all the rest of the Internet network from there. In no time at all, you will be running your computer like a pro.

One other thing - you should defragment (defrag) your computer every two months or so. The way you do this is to click on *Start* on the bottom of the screen, go to *Programs*, then to *Accessories*, then *System Tools,* then finally to *Disk Defrag.* You should do this at night, and leave it on all night. Then you just click it off in the morning. This will put all your things on the hard drive back in order.

The next chapter will be about running your computer from beginning to end without any interruptions. There will be, without a doubt, some repeats, to make sure you can follow everything there, without going back to find things I told you about previously.

44

Chapter 10

SUMMING IT UP

This chapter will go over, from start to finish, how I have learned my way. It will tell you about how I did this without a lot of education. To show you the only way I run the computer, and have fun doing it. How I saw sights that I never would have seen if my granddaughter hadn't got me this computer, and how I learned what I know without her giving me any lessons. I have seen things, done things and emailed people all over the world, things that I never would have been able to do without this computer. Since I never could afford to travel, and wouldn't have anyway because I was always afraid to fly, this was a blessing and I hope it will be a blessing for you too.

Just a bird's eye view of running the computer my way - the easy way. First thing is to turn on your computer. Double click on the icon, *Internet Explorer* or whatever your computer says. All computers don't have the same icons with the same name but they perform the same function. Go to *Mail*, then click on *Read Mail* and you are in your email program, ready to exchange messages over the Internet. I gave you, in the previous chapter step-by-step instructions, but any time you want to go on to greater things just back out of your email program, and click right on *Search*. You can find anything you want by typing in the word or subject matter that you want to find, such as groceries or automobiles. When you do this, you will find a long list of web sites; just click on the ones that look good to you. After you do all you want in *Search,* or you're getting tired, leave *Search* by clicking on *Home*. This will take you back to your *Home Page*. There is a X up in the right hand corner, click on it and you are back to the main screen.

"You invested $100 a week ago and we're not rich yet.
I thought you knew how to use a computer!"

If you want to play games just click on *Games* and pick out the one you want to play. One day you might just want to relax and play music. You can do this by clicking on the icon - *Real Player, or QuickTime*. Put a CD in your computer and sit back and relax. When you're ready to quit, just go back to the main screen with the icons, and you are through. It is better not to shut down the computer. Stay on the main screen and leave it alone. The only time you would want to shut down is, when going away for a long visit or in the time of a storm. To do this, click on *Start*, then on *Shutdown*, then hit *OK* and your computer will shut down properly.

Chapter 11

MY TESTIMONIAL

I want to end here with this chapter: To tell you how it came about, after all the heartache and trouble I had when my spouse died. I felt like the last hope of survival had come to an abrupt end. I went into a deep depression. Boredom set in. I became a basket case. I did not want to live any longer. I felt very strongly, that my life was over at the age of eighty-two. But God had other plans for me, as this book shows.

I added this last chapter to give you, the reader, more hope than I had. It will help you, if you fall into a situation like mine. You too can overcome it. I was just lying around, feeling sorry for myself, not realizing that I was hurting my family. My granddaughter saw what was happening to me, so she thought of a way to get my mind off my troubles. That's why she gave me the computer. With it she put tools in my hand, so I'd have to work my brain. This made a new man out of me. That's why I learned this computer, the working of the Internet, email, and all that I wrote about. It has been the biggest challenge of my life. I spent countless hours learning all I know, without any help from anyone.

All because my granddaughter had forethought enough to give me hope once more in my life: Allowing me to show the world that if an eighty-two years old man could do this without education, so can everybody else. I had the fun of my life. Now I feel sixty instead of eighty.

I'm glad I could write this book. I think it can help you, and others too. You too can enjoy life as I have the last year!

"THE COMPUTER SAYS I NEED TO UPGRADE MY BRAIN
TO BE COMPATIBLE WITH ITS NEW SOFTWARE."

USEFUL THINGS TO KNOW

You can find detailed, easy to understand explanations in this section about those features of a computer the author uses every day. These are very useful things to know, when you talk to others about what you do on the Internet, and how. More importantly, you can use them as a reference, in case you need to ask for help. Or just have fun learning more about how your computer works. Here we go!

WHAT THIS "COMPUTER THING" IS REALLY MADE OF

In most cases, the main piece of a personal computer (PC) system today is a box. This is where everything you do gets processed. Your **monitor** with a screen is attached to it, unless it is part of the computer, like in Apple iMacs. So is the **keyboard** that you use to write email messages, letters, and so on. The **mouse** that moves the arrow on the screen, or use to open a program or a file to work with, is also connected to the same box.

In addition, there is a slot for **compact discs** (CDs) that you can use to listen to your favorite music, or play games from. It may come with a tray to put your CD on. If you have an iMac, it is even easier - you just slide the CD in. There may be slots for other disks that are used to transfer computer files and programs around.

You probably have seen flat screen monitors or TVs already. Combining them with a miniaturized computer produces much smaller, yet fully functional units, called notebook computers, web pads, Internet appliances, and so on.

MAIN (ICON) SCREEN

WITH ICONS AND MENUS

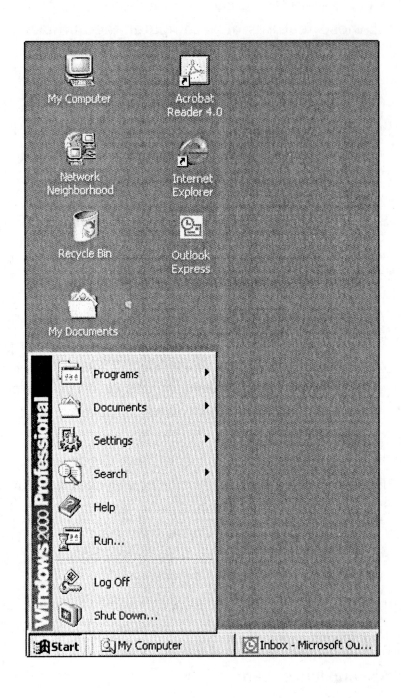

Because they are much easier to use, and cheaper too, there will be more, and more of them, instead of full size personal computers. That doesn't matter to us, since they will still work the same way as the "box."

HARD DRIVE - IN YOUR COMPUTER, NOT THE CAR!

When the author talks about a hard drive, he is really talking about one built into a computer. What he means is a device that stores your email messages, addresses, links to web sites, and so on. It is like our brain's long-term memory, holding all the programs, and your files ready for use when your computer is turned on. The reason we call it a hard drive is, because it is a disk drive encased in a metal box, which cannot be removed from the computer, unlike other disks, such as the much smaller floppy, or Zip disks.

HARD DRIVE - DEFRAG(MENTATION)

As you save messages or other files, they are copied to different locations on the hard drive. Once you have a lot of files all over, your computer will need much more time to find, and rebuild them. The *Defrag* program finds pieces of these files, and puts them together. This speeds up reading your messages, or work with your other files.

MAIN SCREEN (ALSO CALLED ICON SCREEN, OR ICON PAGE)

The first thing you see, when turning on the computer is a bunch of screens from the **operating system**, which is the program that actually runs the computer. These stop after a while, and leave you either with a login box, or the full screen with icons.

If you need to log in, just type in the name and password you got from the person who set up your computer. Once that is done, the main screen becomes fully visible, and you're ready to go.

Icons are nothing else but small images you click on to start programs, such as *Internet Explorer, Netscape Navigator and Messenger, Outlook Express*, and *Real Player*. You can also use them to open files, like the letters you write, but we don't cover that here. Either way, they are very handy to use, and save you a lot of time.

Menus are lists you can use to do what you want, like shutting down your computer, by clicking on the *Start* button, then on *Shut Down.* Every **program** you open up on the screen is in a **window**, which has menus. They work the same way, so once you know how to use one, you know how to work with all others.

When you click on a menu item a drop-down list of commands may appear. It will allow you to open a file, print it, save it, and so on. Also, every program has an icon menu for the most common tasks you need to do, which may be easier to use than the drop-down lists.

YOUR WEB BROWSER PROGRAM

The **Internet** is made up of millions of places, which use standard ways to communicate with each other. The most popular one is called the **World Wide Web**. The *Web*, as it is also called, is very easy to use, because of the web browser program on your computer, which is either *Netscape Navigator*, or *Internet Explorer*. You can go around the world through your browser in minutes, just by clicking on text links, or images. You can also access **web sites** directly, by typing their names into the long box under the icons, called *Location*, or *Address* field.

The first page you see on a web site is called the **home page**, or *home base*, as our author calls it. Your web browser is set to go to this page automatically, when you get a computer. You can ask somebody who knows how to change that to the home page you want to start up with all the time, such as "Hometown Ohio", that the author uses.

WEB BROWSER

NETSCAPE NAVIGATOR, OR INTERNET EXPLORER

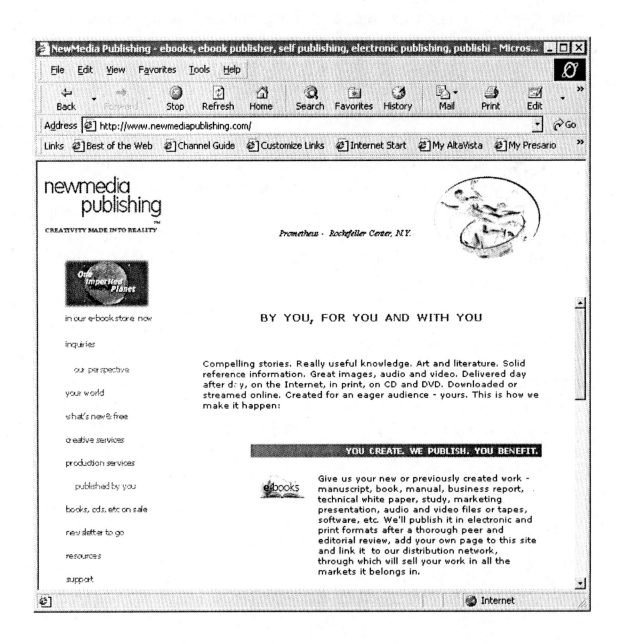

HOW YOUR EMAIL PROGRAM WORKS

The icon *Outlook Express*, or *Outlook*, or any other email program, such as *Eudora*, opens up your email program, when you click on it once, or twice. *Netscape* has its own email too, which is even easier to use, since it is part of the web browser.

Before you can use your email, the program needs to be set up, so it knows which "post office" it has to go to pick up the incoming mail, and to send your outgoing messages. This email service is, generally, part of a package deal from the telephone, cable, or other company like America OnLine. Again, you should ask somebody who knows how to set the email program up, if it has not been done for you yet.

As you can see, email is very similar to regular mail, with two exceptions: It is much, much faster, and cheaper too. That is, because there is no postage - you can exchange messages with anybody all over the world - and because you don't have to take anything to the real post office.

The incoming email messages are like letters you'd receive. They go into the *In-box* folder. You can read them, print them out if a printer is attached to your computer, forward them to other people with your comments, or answer them at any time, by clicking on the *Reply* button. Your replies, or newly composed messages go to the *Out-box* folder if you don't send them out right away, by clicking on, of course, the *Send* button.

You should use the address book of your email program, to type in, and save the names, and email addresses of your loved ones, and everybody else you want to correspond with. These addresses have those funny @ "at" signs in the middle, such as *buck.rogers@aol.com*. Your real, or chosen name is before that sign; your email service provider's name is behind it.

EMAIL

MAIN PROGRAM WINDOW

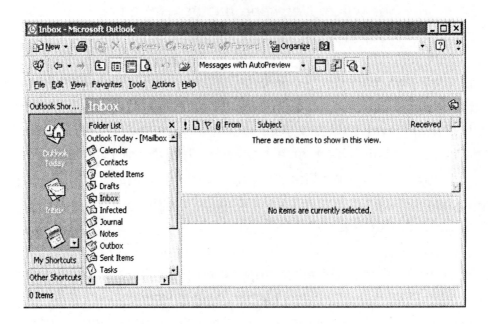

YOUR MESSAGE WINDOW

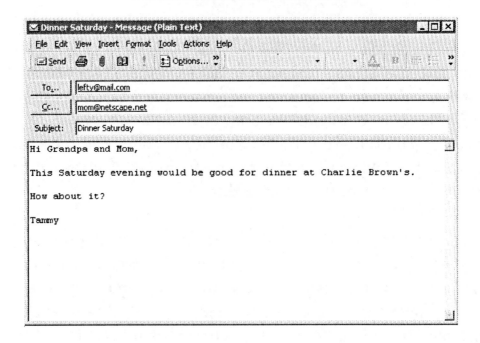

Here is something different from regular mail - when you send an email message, a copy is automatically saved in the **Sent** folder. You can look at it later if you need to, and remove it by using the *Delete* button when you don't care for it anymore. You should also discard old messages in your In-box, when there are too many of them. This is good "housekeeping" practice, which will also make it easy for you to manage your correspondence.

INSTANT MESSAGING

You can also chat - not by voice, but by typing - over the Internet with anybody. This is similar to calling people by phone, in that they have to be online when you are. The most popular instant messaging (IM) services are from America OnLine, and ICQ, which you can access directly through AOL and Netscape now. Other big web sites, like Yahoo and MSN also have popular chat rooms.

MODEM - YOUR CONNECTION TO THE INTERNET

While our author has a great experience with the connection his computer has through his cable TV company, this is not the only, or typical way today. Most of us use the telephone line for that, either as it is, or by having a high-speed digital service line (DSL) installed over it. All of them need one thing - a **modem** - to connect your computer to them. (Similar, more sophisticated devices coming to the market for homes too are called routers). They may be so small that they are built right into the computer, so you don't see anything else but the cords that go in, and out them. As they can be somewhat tricky to set up, you should ask someone who knows the particular type of connection you have in your room, or house to do the installation for you.

CONNECTING TO THE INTERNET

FROM HOME, BY MODEM

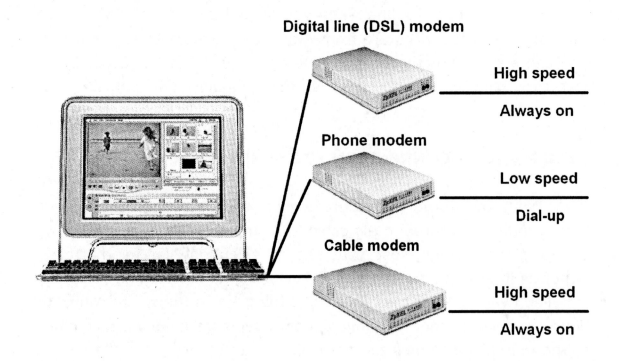

Digital line (DSL) modem

High speed

Always on

Phone modem

Low speed

Dial-up

Cable modem

High speed

Always on

YOUR WORKBOOK

Since this is a "how to" book, we thought it would make sense to provide you with your own space in it. So you have a number of pages in this section to write down what you do, what works, what doesn't, and why. These notes can be very useful to you later, when you want to do something again, or when you need to ask somebody for help. They should come in handy either way, so we urge you to use them as much as possible. Here is the list of them:

A.   THE COMPUTER I HAVE

B.   THE MONITOR, OR FLAT SCREEN IT HAS

C.   THE PRINTER I HAVE HOOKED UP TO IT

D.   AND THE EXTERNAL SPEAKERS IT HAS

E.   MY MODEM - THE LINK TO THE INTERNET

F.   DO I HAVE A WIRELESS CONNECTION?

G.   IF THERE IS ANYTHING ELSE YOU USE

H.   TELL HERE YOUR PROBLEM, AND HOW YOU SOLVED IT

"I'M THE COMPUTER FAIRY. TECHNICAL SUPPORT SENDS ME TO FIX THE WORST PROBLEMS."

A. THE COMPUTER I HAVE

Was made by (name of manufacturer): _____

Is called (the name on it): _____

Has a model number: _____

Date I received it: _____

Was installed by: _____

Whose telephone number is: _____

Whose address is: _____

_____

_____

Whose email address is: _____

OTHER NOTES

_____

_____

_____

_____

_____

_____

© 1998 Randy Glasbergen

"My screen is hard to read. Can I have a bigger monitor?"

B. THE MONITOR, OR FLAT SCREEN IT HAS

Was made by (name of manufacturer): _____

Has a model number: _____

Has a screen size of: _____inches, or _____millimeters

Date I received it: _____

Was installed by: _____

Whose telephone number is: _____

Whose address is: _____

_____

_____

Whose email address is: _____

OTHER NOTES

_____

_____

_____

_____

_____

_____

"WHEN DID THE COMPUTER START WRITING ITSELF A PAYCHECK?"

C. THE PRINTER I HAVE HOOKED UP TO IT

Was made by (name of manufacturer): _____

Has a model number: _____

Date I received it: _____

Was installed by: _____

Whose telephone number is: _____

Whose address is: _____

_____

_____

Whose email address is: _____

Size of paper it uses: _____

OTHER NOTES

_____

_____

_____

_____

_____

_____

"We couldn't afford faster computers,
so we just made them *sound* faster."

D. AND THE EXTERNAL SPEAKERS IT HAS

Were made by (name of manufacturer): _____

Have a model number: _____

Date I received them: _____

Were installed by: _____

Whose telephone number is: _____

Whose address is: _____

_____

_____

Whose email address is: _____

OTHER NOTES

_____

_____

_____

_____

_____

_____

_____

"When I told him we need to increase our bandwidth, he hired six fat tuba players."

E. MY MODEM - THE LINK TO THE INTERNET

Was made by (name of manufacturer): _____

Has a model number: _____

Can receive at: High _____ Medium _____ Slow _____ speed

Can send at: High _____ Medium _____ Slow _____ speed

Its serial number is: _____

Date I received it: _____

Was installed by: _____

Whose telephone number is: _____

Whose address is: _____

_____

_____

Whose email address is: _____

OTHER NOTES

_____

_____

_____

_____

F DO I HAVE A WIRELESS CONNECTION?

To your computer - through what device? : _____

Has a model number: _____

To your printer - through what device? : _____

Has a model number: _____

Date I received it: _____

Was installed by: _____

Whose telephone number is: _____

Whose address is: _____

_____

_____

Whose email address is: _____

OTHER NOTES

_____

_____

_____

_____

_____

"I heard on TV that everyone is getting rich
on the Internet! Is this little slot where
the money comes out?"

G. IF THERE IS ANYTHING ELSE YOU USE

It was made by (name of manufacturer): _____

Is called (the name on it): _____

Has a model number: _____

Date I received it: _____

Was installed by: _____

Whose telephone number is: _____

Whose address is: _____

_____

_____

Whose email address is: _____

OTHER NOTES

_____

_____

_____

_____

_____

_____

"We're not getting anywhere, Mr. Johnson.
Can I have a word with your computer in private?"

H. TELL HERE YOUR PROBLEM
AND
HOW YOU SOLVED IT

THE PROBLEM

_____

_____

_____

YOUR SOLUTION

_____

_____

_____

THE PROBLEM

_____

_____

_____

YOUR SOLUTION

_____

_____

_____

"To insult the rude teller, press 1.
To flirt with the pretty teller, press 2.
To mock the perky teller, press 3...."

H. TELL HERE YOUR PROBLEM
AND
HOW YOU SOLVED IT

THE PROBLEM

_____

_____

_____

YOUR SOLUTION

_____

_____

_____

THE PROBLEM

_____

_____

_____

YOUR SOLUTION

_____

_____

_____

Computer Technical Support Hotline

"Here are a few possible solutions to your computer problems: go for a walk, ride a bike, play ball with your kid, talk to your wife, read a book...."

H. TELL HERE YOUR PROBLEM
AND
HOW YOU SOLVED IT

THE PROBLEM

_____

_____

_____

YOUR SOLUTION

_____

_____

_____

THE PROBLEM

_____

_____

_____

YOUR SOLUTION

_____

_____

_____

"Do you, Jason, take Heather to have and to hold,
to e-mail and to fax, to page and to beep,
until death do you part?"

I. NOTES

NOTES

NOTES

NOTES

NOTES

NOTES

NOTES

NOTES

NOTES

NOTES

NOTES

CREDITS, COPYRIGHTS, AND WEB LINKS

Author: **James W. Hart**

Sponsor: His family, specifically his granddaughter Tammy and his son-in-law Bruce Fleishman

Web links:

The author's web page is at:

http://www.newmediapublishing.com/j_hart/j_hart.html

The author's email address on our web site is:

jhart@newmediapublishing.com

(We forward all pertinent messages to him from this address.)

Publisher:

NewMedia Publishing

31 Franklin Turnpike

Waldwick, NJ 07463, USA

www.newmediapublishing.com

SAN: 253-293X

ISBN: 1-893798-18-6

INDEX

ORDER FORM

Thank you for ordering! We offer the following ways to make this easy for you:

Payment by check or money order

Grandpa and the Computer

Price: $12.95 x ____ number of copies   = $ _____
Shipping and handling for 1 or 2 books   = $ 4.84
                              TOTAL   = $ _____

Name: _____
Street: _____
Town: _____ State/Province: _____
Zip/Postal Code: _____ Country: _____

Please send this order or a copy of it with your payment to:

AIL NewMedia Publishing
Ridgewood, NJ 07451, USA

Payment by credit card

Please visit our store on the Internet to place your order at:
http://www.newmediapublishing.com/tok/grandpa_pc_page.html

Questions and inquiries

Call us at 201.444.5051 between 10 a.m.-5 p.m. EST (New York) time, or send email to: *inquire@newmediapublishing.com*

We look forward to hearing from you!

Printed in the United States
4606